Spending Time with Big Jake

Adapted by Kirsten Larsen
Based on a teleplay by Evelyn A.R. Gabai

PSS!
PRICE STERN SLOAN

Jay Jay The Jet Plane and Big Jake are good friends. At the end of every day, they get together to have some fun. Their favorite place to go is Lightning Bug Lake.

"I hope we're not too late!" said Jay Jay as he and Big Jake taxied up to the lakeshore.

"I think we're just in time!" said Big Jake. The two friends watched as the lightning bugs lit up and flew back and forth over the lake.

"Quick!" said Big Jake. "Make a wish!"
"I wish we could share good times like this forever," said Jay Jay.
"I really like spending time with you."
"I like spending time with you, too, little buddy," said Big Jake.

Later Big Jake and Jay Jay flew back home to Tarrytown Airport.

"Good night, Big Jake," said Jay Jay as he taxied toward the Kids' Hangar.

"Good night, Jay Jay," said Big Jake as he headed farther down the runway.

Big Jake slowed to a stop. He thought to himself, "Maybe Jay Jay would like to join me on my cargo run tomorrow. I'd better go ask him now before he falls asleep."

Big Jake returned to the Kids' Hangar, but when he heard laughter coming from inside, he stopped. He didn't want to interrupt the young planes' fun.

"Hey, Jay Jay," said Herky. "What do you and Big Jake do when you go off together every evening?" Jay Jay's friends were gathered around him.

"Um, well, we just go around," stammered Jay Jay.

"Around where?" asked Tracy.

"Oh, just up to Lightning Bug Lake," Jay Jay said reluctantly. As much as Jay Jay loved his friends, he wanted to keep his special time with Big Jake to himself.

"Really?" Snuffy said excitedly. "Can we go, too?" "We'll make it a real celebration!" said Herky. "We'll invite *everybody*!"

"No! You guys have it all wrong!" exclaimed Jay Jay. "I mean, it's okay when Big Jake and I hang out together, but it's not such a big deal. In fact, you might think it's kind of boring." Jay Jay was relieved to see that his friends believed him.

Meanwhile, Big Jake was still listening outside. He was surprised to hear Jay Jay's words.

"I don't want my little buddy to be bored," he said as he headed home to the Big Hangar. "I've got to think of something exciting for us to do!"

The next morning, Big Jake decided that instead of taking Jay Jay with him on his usual cargo route, he would take him to a more exciting place.

Jay Jay was disappointed. "I like your cargo run," he told Big Jake.

"Since we know the route by heart, we can fly and talk at the same time," said Jay Jay.

"But last night I found out about an incredible new place," said Big Jake. "I can't wait to share it with you."

"Okay," said Jay Jay. "If you really want to go there, count me in!"

Below the planes appeared a meandering river surrounded by cliffs.

"*Wahoo!*" shouted Big Jake. "We're going to race the river! Isn't this fun?"

"I guess," said Jay Jay as the two planes zoomed through the air. Jay Jay enjoyed racing with Big Jake, but he still missed just talking to his best buddy.

The two planes had flown over the river for a long time when suddenly Jay Jay called out, "Oh, no!" His engine started to sputter and choke.

"What's wrong?" asked Big Jake.

"We were having so much fun that I forgot to check my fuel gauge. I'm running out of gas!" he said as he started to slow down.

"Jay Jay, are you alright?" called out Big Jake.

"I'm fine," said Jay Jay, who had landed softly on the river.

"Hold on!" said Big Jake. "I'll drop a cable to you and tow you home." Big Jake was sad. This was not the big adventure he'd had in mind.

The two friends returned to Tarrytown Airport.
   Jay Jay was disappointed that they wouldn't be able to go to Lightning Bug Lake that evening because his parts were wet.
   After the friends said their good-byes, Big Jake thought to himself, "Jay Jay seemed quiet. He must still be bored. I've just *got* to think of something even more exciting for us to do!"

The following morning, Big Jake tried to take Jay Jay on another exciting adventure.

"I'm glad you decided to come with me to Crystal Cave," said Big Jake. "This will be our most spectacular adventure of all—I promise!"

"If you say so, Big Jake," Jay Jay said with a sigh. He wanted to have his quiet time back with Big Jake.

The planes taxied into the Crystal Cave and looked around.
The walls were covered with sparkling crystals.

As the friends waited, the sun rose high in the sky. Sunrays hit
the crystals, lighting up the cave with a dazzling array of colors.

As the friends were admiring the rainbow of colors, dark clouds rolled across the sky. Then rain began to fall and the beautiful colors disappeared.

"Well, it *was* pretty while it lasted," said Jay Jay with a shiver.

"I suppose," Big Jake said with disappointment. "We'd better head back to the airport and get dry . . . again."

By the end of the day, the skies had cleared up. The two friends headed over to Lightning Bug Lake.

As they flew, Big Jake apologized that all his plans had ended in disaster. Little wonder, he said, that Jay Jay was bored with his company.

Jay Jay said "I was never bored with you. I only told my friends that because I didn't want to share our time together."

"We've been so busy having adventures that we haven't had time to talk," said Jay Jay. "And our talks are what make me feel close to you."

"That's my favorite part of being together, too," said Big Jake. "You know, for two good buddies like us, we should have been more honest."

"Boy, that's for sure!" said Jay Jay. "From now on, I'm always going to be honest with you, Big Jake. You really are my best friend!"

And with that, the two planes flew down to the lake where the lightning bugs were dancing.